"Minna

Classic Enid Blyton Stories

This edition first published in the United Kingdom in 1999 by
Brockhampton Press
20 Bloomsbury Street
London WC1B 3QA
a member of the Hodder Headline PLC Group

Designed and produced for Brockhampton Press by
Open Door Limited
80 High Street, Colsterworth, Lincolnshire NG33 5JA

Colour separation: GA Graphics Stamford
Printed in Singapore

Title: Classic Enid Blyton Stories
ISBN: 1-84186-000-X

Classic

Enid Blyton

Stories

BROCKHAMPTON PRESS

Contents

Contents

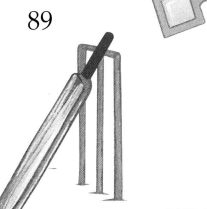

A Spell for a Puppy

There was once a little girl called Joan. She had a great many toys, books and games – almost every one you could think of. You might have thought she would be happy with so many, but she wasn't.

She hadn't the one thing that she really did badly want – and that was a real, live puppy! Her mother didn't like dogs in the house, and would never let her have a puppy, or a kitten either.

"Why do you keep saying you want a puppy to play with?" she often said impatiently to Joan. "You have so many lovely toys. What about your dolls' house? You never play with that now, Joan. Get it out this morning and give it a good clean. Take it out into the garden. It is nice and warm there, and it doesn't matter if you make a mess on the grass."

Joan didn't want to play with her dolls' house. She was not a little girl who was very fond of dolls. She liked running and jumping; she loved animals and birds. She wished she had been a boy. But she was obedient, so she fetched her dolls' house and took it out into the garden. She went down to the hedge at the bottom, where it was sheltered from the wind, for she did not want all the little carpets and curtains to blow away.

She took everything out and cleaned the house well with a wet cloth. She rubbed up the windows, and shook all the carpets. She polished the furniture and put it back again.

It was really a dear little house. There was a nice kitchen downstairs with a sink, and a fine drawing room and small dining room. Upstairs there was a little bathroom with a bath and a basin. Three bedrooms opened out of one another, all papered differently, each with their little carpet on the floor.

"It's a pity, I don't like this sort of toy as most little girls do," thought Joan, as she arranged all the furniture. "I wish I did. But people like different things, I suppose – and I do love animals – and I do wish I had one of my very own."

Just then the dinner-bell rang, and Joan went off to wash her hands and brush her hair. She stood the little house under the hedge out of the sun. She meant to go back after dinner and finish cleaning it outside. The front door knocker wanted a polish, and the chimney wanted washing.

But, after dinner, Mummy said she was going to take Joan out to tea, and the little girl was so pleased that she forgot all about the dolls' house out in the garden. She went off with her mother to catch the bus – and the little house was left under the hedge.

When Joan came back it was late and she was sent to bed at once. She snuggled down under the blankets – and then she suddenly remembered the dolls' house!

"Oh dear!" she said, sitting up in bed. "Whatever would Mummy say if she knew I had left my beautiful dolls' house out-of-doors? I really must go and get it!" She slipped on her dressing gown and went down the stairs. She went out of the garden door and ran down the path.

There was a bright moon and she could see everything quite clearly. She went to the hedge – and then she stopped still in the greatest surprise!

asleep in one of the small beds, a tiny pixie baby. It was really too good to be true. The little girl sighed with delight – and the pixies heard her!

What do you think? There were lights in her little dolls' house – and people were walking about in the rooms – and the front door was wide open!

"Whoever is in there?" thought Joan, in great excitement. She bent down to see – and to her great delight she saw that the little folk inside were pixies with tiny wings. They were running about, talking at the tops of their voices. They sounded like swallows twittering.

Joan looked into one of the bedrooms through the window – and she saw, fast

They slammed the front door at once – and one of them opened a bedroom window and looked out.

"Who are you?" they cried to Joan.

"I'm the little girl this house belongs to," said Joan. "I've been cleaning it to-day, and I left it here and forgot it. What are you doing here?"

"Oh, we found it and thought it would do so nicely for us and our family," said the pixie, in a disappointed voice. "You see, we lived in a nice hollow tree – but the woodmen came and cut it down – and we hadn't a home. Then we came along by your hedge and saw this lovely house. It's just the right size for us and, as there didn't seem to be anyone living in it, we thought we would take it."

"Well, I simply love to see you in it," said Joan. "I do really." "Would you let it to us?" asked the pixie. "We would pay you rent, if you liked."

"Oh, no," said Joan. "I don't want you to pay me for it. You can have it, if you like. I am very lucky to see you and talk to you, I think. I am most excited, really I am!"

"How kind of you to let us have it," said the pixie, beaming all over her little pointed face. "Can't we do something for you in return? Isn't there anything you want very much?"

"Well, yes, there is," said Joan. "I want a puppy dog very, very much. I have wanted one for years. But I have never had one."

"We'll give you a spell for one," said the pixie. She ran downstairs and opened the front door. She held up a very small box to Joan. "Take this," she said. "There is a spell inside. Blow it out of your window to-night and say 'Puppy, puppy, come to me. Make me happy as can be. Puppy, puppy, come to me!'"

"Oh, thank you!" said Joan, more excited than ever. "Listen, pixie. Don't you think I'd better take your house to the woods to-morrow? The gardener often comes here and he might be cross if he saw I'd left my house in the hedge."

"Yes, that's a good idea," said the pixie.

"We would like to be somewhere in the woods. Will you carry the house there to-morrow morning? We'll show you where we'd like it."

"Yes, I will," promised Joan. "Now, I must go. Good night, and thank you very much."

She ran off, looking back to see the little windows of her dolls' house lighted up so gaily. She went up to her bedroom and opened the small box. She took out the spell, which was like a tiny bit of thistle-down, and blew it out of the window.

"Puppy, puppy, come to me. Make me happy as can be. Puppy, puppy, come to me!" she whispered.

Then she got into bed and fell fast asleep.

And whatever do you think happened next morning? Why, her Uncle Joe came to stay, and with him he brought a small, fat brown puppy in a basket – a present for Joan!

"Here you are!" he said to the delighted little girl. "I know you've always wanted a pup – and you shall have one! His name is Sandy – treat him well, and he'll be a good friend to you!"

Joan was full of joy. She loved the puppy, and it licked her nose and hands, pleased to have such a nice little mistress. She raced down the bottom of the garden with the puppy at her heels. The dolls' house was still there, and outside stood all the pixies, waiting for her to come.

"I've got my puppy, I've got my puppy!" she said, joyfully. "The spell worked! Now, I'll carry your house to the woods!"

She picked it up and carried it off, the pixies half flying, half running in front to show her the way. She put it down in a little glade by the side of a small stream and said good-bye once more. Then she and Sandy raced home again, a very happy pair.

And if you should happen to come across a dolls' house in the woods, don't touch it, will you? It will be the one belonging to the pixies! They still live there, you see!

Jinky's Joke

Once there was a wicked little pixie called Jinky. He was always playing jokes on people, and sometimes they were funny, but more often they were not.

One week he went to all the shops that sold pails and saucepans and ordered dozens to be sent to old Dame Cooky. Well, the poor old lady couldn't *imagine* why so many saucepans and pails kept arriving, and she really grew quite frightened when she saw her kitchen piled up from floor to roof with them. It took her two whole days to take them back to the shops and explain that she hadn't ordered them.

Another time, Jinky put glue on the big wooden seat that stood outside the town hall. People sat there and waited for the bus. Oh dear, how angry everyone was when the bus came by and they got up – because they left half their skirts behind them!

Now one day Jinky found a few tins of paint as he passed the builder's yard. He tucked them under his arm with a grin. He meant to borrow some of that paint.

He stole into Mother Creaky's back-garden and called her hens to him. He painted those poor hens with the paint out of the tins till they looked like feathered rainbows!

"Oh, Henny-Penny, you do look queer!" said Jinky, laughing as he set free a hen with a red beak, a yellow comb, a purple tail, green wings, and blue legs. And certainly the hen did look very strange. All the other hens looked at her, and then they ran at her and began to peck her, for they thought she was a stranger.

One by one, Jinky painted all the poor hens, and left them squabbling and pecking one another, for they couldn't bear to see such strange-looking creatures. Then Jinky heard Mother Creaky coming, and he hid behind the fence and watched.

"Oh! What's this I see?" cried Mother Creaky, in great astonishment, when she came to her gate. "Are these hens – or are they parrots or kingfishers? Never did I see such colours in my life!"

"Cluck, cluck, cluck!" said the hens sadly, and they ran to their mistress. They rubbed against her skirt and made it red, blue, green, orange, yellow, and purple.

"Oh, you poor creatures!" she cried. "Someone has painted you! You'll all have to be bathed."

Well, of course, hens hate the water, and Mother Creaky got pecked and scratched when she tried to get the paint off their feathers. She heard Jinky chuckling behind the fence, and caught sight of him running away. She was very angry.

"So that's Jinky again, is it?" she grumbled. "Well, it's time he got a fright. He left behind these paints – and I'll just go along to his house and do a little painting myself. I know he goes to supper with Higgle to-night. I shall have a nice time before he goes home."

So Mother Creaky picked up the tins of paint and went along to Jinky's cottage. The front door was black, with a letterbox and a knocker above it. Mother Creaky set to work.

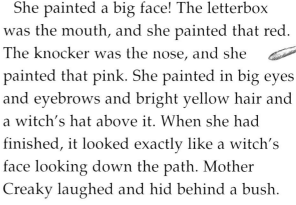

She painted a big face! The letterbox was the mouth, and she painted that red. The knocker was the nose, and she painted that pink. She painted in big eyes and eyebrows and bright yellow hair and a witch's hat above it. When she had finished, it looked exactly like a witch's face looking down the path. Mother Creaky laughed and hid behind a bush.

The night came and the moon shone out brightly. Jinky came home, whistling, laughing whenever he thought of Mother Creaky's hens.

He turned in at his gate – and then he saw the painted face looking at him from his front door!

"Owwwwww!" cried Jinky in fright. "Ooooooh! Owwwwww! What is it? What is it?"

Then Mother Creaky spoke in a deep voice from behind her bush. It seemed to poor Jinky as if the face on his door were speaking, and he listened in fright.

"Jinky!" said the deep voice. "How dare you play tricks on my friend, Mother Creaky! How dare you upset poor Dame Cooky! I have come to punish you!"

"Oh, please don't, please don't!" wept Jinky. "I won't play tricks again. I didn't know that Dame Cooky and Mother Creaky had a witch for a friend. Please forgive me."

"I will only forgive you if you promise not to play unkind tricks any more," answered the deep voice.

"I promise, I promise!" sobbed Jinky, trembling so much that he could hardly stand.

"Very well. You may come into your house and I will not harm you," said the voice. But Jinky didn't dare to go in. No – he turned and fled away. He spent the night most uncomfortably in a dry ditch, with beetles and spiders crawling all over him.

And in the morning when he crept back to his house, his front door was just the same as usual! You see, Mother Creaky, with many giggles and chuckles, had washed away the witch's face with turpentine and water.

"He'll think twice before he plays a silly trick again," she said.

And Jinky did think twice. He didn't tell a single person about the witch he had seen – but Dame Creaky told the ice-cream man, and he told me – so that's how *I* know!

Visitors in the Night

The toys were very tired. They had had a very exciting day because the children had friends to tea – and all the toys had been played with.

"I simply can't keep my eyes open," said the pink cat. "It's no use. I must go to sleep."

"So must I," said the curly-haired doll. "I've been undressed and dressed so often today that I feel quite worn-out. I shall get into my cot and go to sleep."

And so, when somebody came into the playroom in the middle of the night, nobody was awake! The bear was giving tiny little snores in his corner, and the pink cat was all curled up in hers.

Somebody pattered in from a hole behind the cupboard, and squeaked loudly: "A message! I bring a message!"

Nobody answered. Nobody saw the small brown mouse with the twitching nose and long whiskers. He stood there in the middle of the floor, looking round in surprise.

"Isn't anyone awake?
I bring a message.
A MOST important
message."

Still nobody woke up. The mouse looked for his best friend there – Clicky, the clockwork mouse. Ah, there he was. He ran over to him and pulled his tail hard.

"Clicky! Wake up! I've got a MESSAGE!"

Clicky woke up with a jump. "Dear me! What are you pulling my tail like that for?" he squealed.

"I've got a message from the five little fairies who live in Bluebell Wood," said the mouse, excitedly. "They came to a party given by the pixie who lives in our garden and, oh dear, they've fallen in the pond!"

"Goodness!" said the clockwork mouse. "Are they wet?"

"Yes, they're soaked through," said the real mouse. "And they sent me here with a message. Can the dolls' house dolls let them sleep in the dolls' house tonight? They simply *must* dry themselves, and get to bed, else they will have dreadful colds."

"I'll wake up the little dolls," said Clicky at once and soon he was knocking at the dolls' house door *rat-a-tat-a-tat*! The little mother-doll answered the door in her night-dress, most surprised.

When she heard about the wet fairies, she was quite upset. "The poor things! Mouse, go and bring them here at once. Are they small enough to come up your hole? They are? That's good. Then they will be small enough to sleep in the beds in my little dolls' house."

Off went the mouse at once, and the dolls' house dolls began to be very busy indeed. They ran water in the little bath – they put out clean towels – they made the beds and warmed blankets by the tiny kitchen fire. What excitement there was!

Soon five wet, miserable little fairies came trooping out of the mousehole with the mouse leading them. All the toys welcomed them, because Clicky had told them the news, of course. They were all awake now, and anxious to make the tiny fairies happy.

"It's so kind of you." Said Tippitty, the biggest fairy. "We're so wet and cold!"

The mother-doll welcomed them into the dolls' house at once. "A hot bath for you!" she said. "And warm beds. And we'll give you hot soup to drink when you're in bed. I'll dry your clothes while you're asleep."

The five fairies felt much better after a nice hot bath. They wiped themselves dry with the little towels, and then put on nighties belonging to the dolls' house dolls. They fitted them beautifully.

"Into bed with you," said the kind little mother-doll. "Now – here comes your soup!"

Soon the five fairies were drinking hot soup out of the tea-set cups. They felt warm and happy. How lucky they were to find a little house like this, with beds just the right size.

"We shan't get colds now," said Tippitty. "We shall feel quite all right in the morning. Oh, what a comfortable bed this is!"

Soon all five had snuggled down. The mother-doll tucked them up. "Please will you leave the light on?" asked Tippitty. "Just in case we wake up and have forgotten where we are!"

So the lights were left on in the little house – and the toys came creeping to the windows to peep in.

"Look – there they are, tucked up in the little dolls' beds," whispered the toy soldier. "Aren't they sweet?"

"They are just the right size," said the pink cat. "Aren't we lucky to have five fairies sleeping here tonight? It is a very great honour."

They crept back to the toy cupboard and fell asleep again. The dolls' house dolls went to sleep too. Everyone was really very tired.

They didn't wake up till quite late. One of the children came scampering in at eight o'clock, on her way down to breakfast. She stopped in surprise when she saw the dolls' house.

"Why! The lights are on!" she cried. "Jane! Come and see! Somebody has left the dolls' house lights on!"

Jane came running in too. "Goodness, Eileen – who could have left them on?" she said. "I know we turned them off last night. Let's look inside and see if anything has gone wrong with them."

Good gracious me! What a to-do there was in the dolls' house when the dolls heard the children outside! The mother-doll woke the five fairies at once.

"Quick! You must dress and go," she said. "The children are here – they may catch you and take you to school to show their friends!"

But there wasn't time to dress – Jane and Eileen were looking through the windows – and they saw the five fairies hopping out of bed in a hurry.

They stared as if they couldn't believe their eyes. Then they ran to their mother's room. "Mummy! Mummy, do come! There are fairies in our dolls' house! Come quickly. They're the prettiest things you ever saw!"

But when their mother came to the playroom and went to look in at the windows, there were no fairies to be seen!

They had caught up their clothes, fled down the little dolls' house stairs, run across the floor, and disappeared down the mousehole at top speed. Tippitty fell over her night-dress, but picked herself up just in time.

"Oh! There's nobody here now!" said Jane in dismay.

"There never was," said Mummy, laughing. "It was just a joke of yours."

"It wasn't!" said Eileen. "And look, the front door is open now – and see, one of the fairies has dropped a little petticoat as she ran! Oh, what a pretty, cobwebby thing!"

She showed her mother the tiny petticoat. Tippitty had dropped it without knowing.

"Well – it's a most extraordinary thing – and I don't really believe it!" said Mummy. "Now, do come and have your breakfast. Bring the tiny petticoat to show Daddy, if you like – but he won't believe your tale either."

He didn't, of course – but he would have if he had peeped in at the playroom the next night, and had seen five small fairies tripping out of the mousehole with parcels under their arms – the night-dresses belonging to the dolls' house dolls, all beautifully washed and ironed!

"Thank you for your help last night," said Tippitty. "And here are the night-dresses you lent us – and also a little magic spell in a box. It will grant you any wish you like – but only one – so think carefully before you use it!"

Well, what a surprise – a magic wish of their own! They simply can't wait to use it – and I really do wonder what they will wish for, don't you?

Thirteen O'clock

Once upon a time Sandy was walking home from school when he saw an extra fine dandelion clock.

"What a beauty!" he said, picking it with its stalk. "I wonder if it will tell me the right time."

He blew it – puff! A cloud of white fluffy seeds flew away. There were plenty left on the clock. He blew again – puff! More fluff flew away on the breeze. Puff! Puff! Puff! He counted as he blew.

"One o'clock! Two o'clock! Three! Four! Five! Six o'clock! Seven! Eight! Nine! Ten! Eleven o'clock! Twelve o'clock! *Thirteen o'clock!*"

At the thirteenth puff there was no fluff left on the dandelion clock at all. It was just an empty stalk.

And then things began to happen. A noise of little voices was heard, and Sandy looked down at his feet. Round him was a crowd of pixies, shouting loudly.

"Did you say thirteen o'clock? Hi, did you say thirteen o'clock?"

"Yes" said Sandy, in astonishment. "The dandelion clock said thirteen o'clock."

"Oh my goodness me, thirteen o'clock only happens once in a blue moon!" cried the biggest pixie. "Whatever shall we do?"

"Why, what's the matter?" asked Sandy. "What are you so upset about?"

"Don't you know?" shouted all the pixies together. "Why, at thirteen o'clock all the witches from Witchland fly on broomsticks, and if they see any elf, pixie, brownie or gnome out of Fairyland they catch them and take them away. Oh dear, goodness gracious, whatever shall we do?"

Sandy felt quite alarmed. "Do they take little boys, too?"he asked.

"We don't know, but they might," answered the biggest pixie. "Hark! Can you hear the Witches' Wind blowing?"

Sandy listened. Yes, a wind was blowing up, and it sounded a funny sort of wind, all whispery and strange.

"That's the wind the witches use to blow their broomsticks along," said the pixies. "Little boy, you'd better run home quickly."

But Sandy wasn't going to leave the little pixies alone. They were frightened, so he felt he must stay and look after them. "I'll stay with you," he said. "But do you think you could make me as small as you, because if I'm as big as this the witches will see me easily and catch me."

"That's easy to do," said the biggest pixie. "Shut your eyes, put your hands over your ears and whisper 'Hoona-looki-allo-pie' three times to yourself. Then you'll be as small as we are. When you want to get big again do exactly the same, but say the magic words backwards."

Sandy felt excited. He shut his eyes and covered his ears with his hands. Then he whispered the magic words three times – and lo and behold, when he opened his eyes again he was as small as the pixies! They crowded round him, laughing and talking.

"I am Gobbo," said the biggest one, "and this is my friend, Twinkle."

Sandy solemnly shook hands with Gobbo and Twinkle. Then, as the wind grew louder, the pixies crowded together in alarm, and looked up at the sky.

"Where shall we go to hide?" said Twinkle. "Oh, quick, think of somewhere, somebody, or the witches will be along and will take us prisoners!"

Everybody thought hard, and then Sandy had a good idea.

"As I came along I noticed an old saucepan thrown away in the hedge," he said. "Let's go and find it and get under it. It will hide us all beautifully."

Off went all the pixies, following Sandy. He soon found the saucepan, and by pushing hard they managed to turn it upside-down over them, so that it quite hid them. There was a hole in the side out of which they could peep. "I've dropped my handkerchief," suddenly cried Twinkle, pointing to where a little red hanky lay on the ground some way off. "I must go and get it."

"No, don't," said Gobbo. "You'll be caught. The witches will be along any minute now. Hark how the wind is blowing!"

"But I must get it!" cried Twinkle. "If I don't the witches will catch sight of it out there, and down they'll all come to see what it is. Then they'll sniff pixies nearby and come hunting under this saucepan for us."

"Ooooooooh!" groaned all the pixies, in fright. "Well, go and get it quickly!" said Gobbo to Twinkle. "Hurry up!"

Twinkle crept out from under the saucepan and everybody watched him anxiously. The wind grew louder and louder and all the tall grasses

swayed like trees in the wind. Then there came a sort of voice in the wind and Sandy listened to hear what it said.

"The witches are coming, the witches are coming!" it said, in a deep-down, grumbling sort of voice, rushing into every hole and corner. Sandy peeped through the hole in the saucepan to see what Twinkle was doing. He was dodging here and there between the grasses. At last he reached the place where his red handkerchief lay, and he picked it up and put it into his pocket.

And then, oh my goodness, the pixies in the saucepan saw the first witches coming! They shouted to Twinkle, and he looked up in the sky. There they were, three witches in pointed hats and long cloaks, sitting on long broomsticks, flying through the cloudy sky.

"Quick, Twinkle, quick!" yelled Sandy and the pixies. How they hoped the witches wouldn't see him! He crouched down under a yellow buttercup till they were past, and then began to run to the saucepan.

"There are two more witches coming!" shouted the pixies, pointing. Sure enough, two more could be seen in the windy sky, much lower down than the others. Twinkle crept under a green stinging-nettle and stayed there without movement till the witches had gone safely by.

"Poor Twinkle! He *will* be stung!" said Gobbo, sadly. When the two witches were past Twinkle ran from beneath the nettle straight to the saucepan and crept underneath in safety. How glad all the pixies were! They crowded round him and stroked his nettle-stung hands and face.

"Never mind, Twinkle, you're safe here," they said.

"Look at all the witches now!" cried Sandy peeping through the hole. "Oh my! What a wonderful sight! I'm glad I'm seeing this."

It certainly was a marvellous sight! The sky was simply full of flying witches, and some of them had black cats sitting in front of them on the broomsticks. The cats coiled their tails round the sticks and held on like monkeys. It was funny to see them.

"Does this always happen at thirteen o'clock?" asked Sandy.

"Always," said Twinkle, solemnly. "But thirteen o'clock only happens once in a blue moon, as I told you before. The moon must have been blue this month. Did you notice it?"

"Well, no, I didn't," said Sandy. "I'm nearly always in bed when it's moonlight. Oh I say! Look! One of the witches has lost her black cat!"

The pixies peeped out of the hole in the saucepan. Sure enough, one of the black cats had tumbled off its broomstick. It had tried to be clever and wash itself on the broomstick, and had lost its hold and tumbled off. It was falling through the air, and the witch was darting down with her broomstick, trying her best to catch it.

She just managed to grab hold of the cat before it fell on the ground – but her broomstick was smashed to pieces, and the witch rolled over and over on the grass, holding the cat safely in her arms. She sat up and looked round. When she saw her broken broomstick she began to howl.

"It's broken. It's broken! I'll never be able to fly back home! Boo hoo hoo!"

Sandy was frightened to see the witch rolling over and over. He thought she would be sure to hurt herself. He was a very kind-hearted boy, and he longed to go and ask her if she was all right. He began to squeeze himself under the saucepan, meaning to go and see if the witch was hurt. But the pixies tried to pull him back.

"Don't go, don't go," they whispered, for the witch was quite near. "She'll change you into a black-beetle."

"Why should she?" asked Sandy. "I'm going to be kind to her. Besides, she's got a nice face, rather like my granny's – I'm sure she isn't a bad witch."

He wriggled himself away from the hands of the pixies and ran over to the witch. She was sitting down on the grass crying big tears all down her cheeks. The cat was on her lap, still looking frightened.

The witch was most surprised to see him. Sandy stopped just by her. She had a very tall pointed hat, a long cloak round her shoulders, with silver suns, moons and stars all over it. The cat arched its back and spat angrily at the little boy.

"Excuse me," said Sandy, politely. "I saw you roll over on the ground when your broomstick broke, and I came to see if you were hurt."

"Well," said the witch, holding out her left hand, "I'm not much hurt – but my hand is a bit cut. I must have hit it against a stone when I rolled over."

"I'll tie it up for you with my handkerchief." Said Sandy. "It's quite clean."

The witch looked more astonished than ever. She held out her hand and Sandy tied it up very neatly.

"Thank you," said the witch. "That's most kind of you. Oh dear – just look at my poor broomstick – it's broken in half! I shall never get back to Witchland again!"

Sandy looked at the broomstick. The broom part was all right, but the stick was broken. Sandy felt in his pocket to see if he had brought his knife with him. Yes, he had!

"I'll cut you another stick from the hedge," he said. "Then you can fit it into the broomhead and use it to fly away with!"

"You're the cleverest, kindest boy I ever met!" said the witch. "Thank you so much! Most people are afraid of witches, you know, because they think we will change them into black-beetles, or something – but that's an old-fashioned idea. The old witches *were* like that but nowadays we witches are decent folk, making magic spells that will do no-one any harm at all."

"Well, I'm glad to hear *that*!" said Sandy, hoping that the pixies under the saucepan were hearing it, too. He went to the hedge and cut another stick for the witch. He fitted it neatly into the broomhead and threw away the broken stick. The witch was very pleased.

She said a magic spell over it to make it able to fly. Then she turned to Sandy.

"Won't you have a ride with me?" she asked. "It is great fun. I will see that you are safe."

"Ooh, I'd *love* a ride!" cried Sandy, in delight. "But you are sure you won't take me away to Witchland?"

"I told you that witches don't do horrid things now," said the witch. "Do I *look* like a nasty witch?"

"No, you don't," said Sandy. "Well, I'll come for a ride – I'd love to! I'll be awfully late for my dinner but an adventure like this doesn't come often!"

He perched himself on the broomstick, behind the witch, who took her black cat on her knee. Just as they were about to set off, there came a great clatter, and the saucepan nearby was overturned by the pixies. They streamed out, shouting and calling.

"Take us for a ride, too! Take us for a ride, too!"

The witch looked at them in amazement. She had no idea that any pixies were near. She laughed when she saw where they had been hiding.

"Climb up on the stick," she said. "I'll give you a ride, too!"

Goodness, there wasn't room to put a blade of grass on that broomstick after all the pixies had climbed up on it! What a squash there was, to be sure!

The witch called out a string of magic words and the broomstick suddenly flew up into the air with a jerk. Sandy held on tightly. The pixies yelled in delight and began to sing joyfully. All the other witches flying high in the sky laughed to see such a crowded broomstick. Sandy did enjoy himself. He was very high up, and the wind whistled in his ears and blew his hair straight back from his head.

"Now we're going down again!" said the witch, and the broomstick swooped downwards. It landed gently and all the pixies tumbled off in a heap. Sandy jumped off and thanked the witch very much for such a lovely ride.

"I must go now," she said. "The hour of thirteen o'clock is nearly over and I must return to Witchland. Good-bye, kind little boy, and I'll give you another ride next time it's thirteen o'clock. If you wait for me here, I'll take you all the way to Witchland and back!"

Off she went, she and her black cat, and left Sandy standing on the grass, watching her fly away. The pixies waved to the witch and she waved back. "Well, that *was* an adventure!" cried the pixies. "We'll never be afraid of witches again, that's certain! Hooray!"

"I wonder what the time is," said Sandy. "What comes after thirteen o'clock? Is it fourteen o'clock?"

"Oh no!" said Twinkle. "Thirteen o'clock just comes and goes. It isn't any time really. It always comes after twelve o'clock, but it's followed by one o'clock as if nothing had happened in between!"

Somewhere a church clock chimed the hour. Sandy listened. Then the clock struck one, and no more.

"One o'clock, one o'clock!" cried the pixies their voices growing very small and faint. "Thirteen o'clock is over! Good-bye, good-bye!"

Sandy looked at them – they were vanishing like the mist, and in a moment or two he could see nothing of them. They just weren't there.

"I must make myself big again," he thought. He remembered the words quite well. He shut his eyes and covered up his ears. He had to say the magic words backwards, so he thought hard before he spoke.

"Pie-allo-looki-hoona!" he said. When he opened his eyes he was his own size again! He set off home, running as fast as he could, for he was afraid that his mother would be wondering where he was.

He ran into the house and found his mother just putting out his dinner. She didn't seem to think he was late at all!

"You're just in nice time," she said to Sandy. "Good boy! You must have come straight from school without stopping!"

"But mother – ever such a lot has happened since I left school," said Sandy in surprise. "I'm dreadfully late!"

"No, darling, it's only just gone one o'clock," said his mother, looking at the clock.

"Didn't *you* have thirteen o'clock, too, this morning?" asked Sandy, sitting down to his dinner.

"What *are* you talking about?" said his mother with a laugh. "Thirteen o'clock! Whoever heard of that? That only happens in Fairyland, once in a blue moon, I should think!"

Sandy thought about it. Perhaps it was true – perhaps thirteen o'clock belonged to the fairies, and not to the world of boys and girls. How lucky he had been to have that one magic hour of thirteen o'clock with the pixies and the witch. And next time it was thirteen o'clock he was going to ride on a broomstick again. Oh, what fun!

"I do hope it will be thirteen o'clock again soon," he said.

"Eat up your dinner and don't talk nonsense!" said his mother, laughing.

But it wasn't nonsense, was it? Sandy is going to blow all the dandelion clocks he sees so that he will know when it is thirteen o'clock again. If you blow them too, you may find that magic hour as well!

The Little Musical Box

In the playroom was a dear little musical box. It was quite round, and it had a handle that could be turned. When you turned the handle, the music played.

"Tiddley-iddley-oh-lee-oh," went the music, and the toys danced to it night after night.

"It's funny to think that music is shut up in this box, isn't it?" said the little doll in the blue dress. "I do like it."

The goldfish in the big glass bowl up on the window-sill tapped a nose against the glass. That meant that he wanted to speak to the toys. So the toy soldier climbed up to listen.

"Bring the music up here," said the goldfish, in his bubbly voice. "I want to hear it too."

So the toy soldier and the teddy carried the little round box carefully up to the goldfish bowl. The bear turned the handle and the music played merrily. "Tiddley-idd-ley, oh-lee-oh!" "Oh, it's lovely!" said the goldfish and he waved his tail about in time to the music. "Please do sometimes bring it to the window-sill for me to hear."

The toys never played the music until it was night-time, and the three children were in bed. They loved Freda, Mollie and John, and were always excited when they came to play with them. But when they were in bed and asleep it would never do to make a noise and wake them up.

The toy soldier always pushed the door almost shut when they played the musical box at night, or raced round the floor in the little clockwork engine. They really had fun then, especially if the engine-driver was in a good temper and

let some of them drive the engine themselves.

One night, when the toys were playing together, there came a great wind that blew outside, and made the trees sway and bend. "Listen to that!" said the bear. "What a noise!"

"I can hear the rain on the window now," said the little black doll. "Drip-drip-drip, drop-drop-drop!"

"And I can feel it!" said the toy soldier suddenly. "Goodness, where's my umbrella?"

"Don't be silly! The window is shut," said the bear.

"Well, it isn't – look, the wind has blown it open," said the black doll. "I can

feel the rain coming in too. And just see how the curtains are blowing!"

The wind had blown so hard that the window had been jerked wide open! It was swinging to and fro, and the curtains were flapping wildly.

The goldfish in his bowl up on the window-sill was frightened. He tapped on the glass with his nose. "The curtain is flapping against my bowl!" he said, in his little bubbling voice. "I'm afraid!"

"Goodness! I hope the curtains don't overturn his bowl!" said the toy soldier – and do you know, just as he had said

that, the wind blew the curtains so hard that they pushed the goldfish bowl right over!

Crash! It tipped on its side and all the water poured out of it in a rush, splashing down the wall to the floor below.

"The goldfish! He's been tipped out too!" cried the black doll. "Oh, Goldie! Are you hurt?"

The little fish was flapping about on the carpet, panting for breath. "I can't breathe when I'm out of water!" he said. "Water! Put me in water! Quick!"

But there wasn't any water to put him in. There wasn't even a vase of flowers he could be slipped into! The toys were in a terrible worry about him.

"He can't breathe! Water, water!" cried the bear. But it wasn't a bit of good shouting out for water. The bathroom was a long way away and water didn't come by itself!

"We'll carry him to the bathroom!" said the doll in the blue dress. "Perhaps there is some water in the bath."

But, you know, the goldfish was so very slippery that nobody could hold him. He just slipped out of their hands, and flapped back on to the carpet again.

And then the toy soldier had a wonderful idea. "Where's the musical box? Let's carry it into the children's bedroom and play it as fast as we can!"

"Oh yes – then they'll wake up and come and see what's happening!" cried the bear. "They'll see poor old Goldie!"

The toy soldier and the bear took hold of the musical box and carried it out of the door, down the passage and in at the door of the children's bedroom. It felt very heavy to them, because they weren't very big.

They put it down on the bedroom floor with a bump. "Now!" said the bear, and he took hold of the handle. He turned it quickly and the music came tinkling out, loud and clear and sweet.

"Tiddley-iddley-oh-lee-oh! Tiddley-iddley-oh-lee-oh!" The musical box played its little tune on and on, and the toy soldier and bear took turns at winding the handle round and round.

Freda woke up first. She sat up, surprised. "Why – it sounds like the musical box!" she said, and she woke up John and Mollie. They sat up and heard it too.

Mollie switched on her torch – and there, in its light, she saw the bear and the toy soldier with the musical box, playing it without stopping!

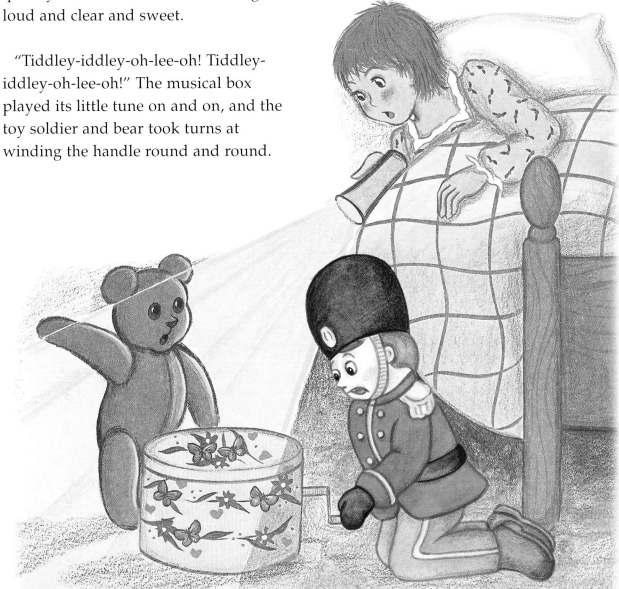

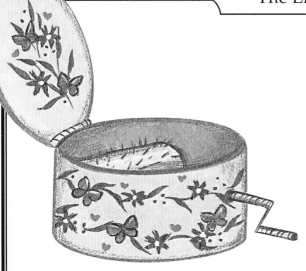

He flapped feebly and turned on his side. The children and the toys watched him, hardly daring to breathe. Would Goldie be all right?"

He turned the right way up again. He moved his fins more strongly. His mouth opened and shut as he took in the water he had missed so much. He gasped a few words in his little bubbly voice. "Thank you! I'll be all right now!"

"Well!" said Freda, in surprise, looking round at the toys, "WHO had the bright idea of waking us up with the musical box so that we could save poor Goldie? You are very good, clever toys – and tomorrow we will give a party for you, just to show you how grateful we are!"

They shut the window tightly so that the wet curtains hung still and straight. The bowl would not be knocked over again!

"Look! Oh look! It's Teddy and the toy soldier with our musical box!" cried Mollie. "Why have they brought it here?"

Just as she said that, the toy soldier and Teddy lifted the musical box and hurried out of the room, hoping the children would follow them to the playroom.

They did, of course – and the very first thing they saw was poor old Goldie flapping very feebly on the floor. He was in a very bad way now, and the children had only just come in time.

"Goldie! You're out of your bowl! Oh look – the wind blew the window open, and the curtains must have knocked over the bowl!" cried John.

Mollie took the bowl and ran to the bathroom. She filled it with water and ran back. John picked up poor Goldie very gently and slid him into the bowl.

"Good night," said the children, and went back to bed – and in the morning they wondered if they had dreamed it all!

"No – we couldn't have," said John. "We couldn't possibly all dream the same dream. Anyway – if it's really true we'll find the carpet wet, where the water was spilt from Goldie's bowl last night."

It *was* wet, of course, so they knew it had all really happened. And now they are giving a grand party for the toys!

Real biscuits! Real lemonade poured out of the teapot! Real bits of chocolate! Well – the toys had never enjoyed a party so much before.

Just look at them, having a good time – and even Goldie isn't forgotten. The toy soldier is dropping a bit of biscuit into his bowl!

The Dumpy Wizard's Party

The Dumpy Wizard was just like his name – fat and round and dumpy. He was a nice old fellow, as merry as a blackbird, and he simply loved giving parties.

People loved going to his parties too! They were so jolly – always lots of nice things to eat and exciting games to play.

But the Dumpy Wizard was very particular about the people he invited to his parties. He wouldn't have anyone greedy. So, if someone was left out of one of his parties, people always knew there was something wrong with them just then.

Now one day Tricky the gnome was running down the street, and he turned the corner quickly. Bump! He banged right into Dumpy the Wizard, and they both fell over. Dumpy sat in a puddle. Tricky banged his head against a wall.

"What did you do that for?" roared Dumpy.

"What do you mean?" yelled back Tricky. "You bumped into me as much as I bumped into you!"

"Why don't you look where you are going?" shouted Dumpy.

"I was, but you came where I was just about to go!" cried Tricky.

"Don't be silly," said Dumpy, drying himself with his handkerchief.

"I'm not," said Tricky.

"Oh yes, you are!" said Dumpy.

"Oh no, I'm not!" said Tricky.

"Oh yes, you are!" said Dumpy. "I shan't ask you to my next party."

"I shall come all the same – yes, and eat up your nicest jellies!" said Tricky.

"You won't," said Dumpy.

"Oh yes, I will," said Tricky.

"Oh no, you won't," said Dumpy.

"Now then, move on, you two," said Blueboy, the policeman of the village. "Stop quarrelling!"

So Tricky and Dumpy had to move on. Dumpy was quite sure he *wouldn't* let Tricky come to his party – and Tricky was quite sure he *would* go – and eat up the best jellies too!

Dumpy sent out his invitations – and do you know, everyone was invited this time – except Tricky, of course! He said he didn't care, not he! And in his cunning little head he made a plan.

It was to be a fine party. There was to be a gramophone going, and everyone was to sing and dance to it. There were to be four different coloured jellies – green, red, orange and pink – and a fine cake with a rabbit in sugar on the top. Ooooh!

The day soon came. Everyone put on his best clothes and looked as excited as could be. Only Tricky kept on his old clothes, but he didn't seem to care one bit – he just ran about as usual, humming and whistling as if *he* didn't care about parties.

Four o'clock came. Gnomes, goblins, brownies, and pixies crowded into Dumpy's little cottage. Only two people were not there – Tricky, of course – and Blueboy the policeman, who had to guard everyone's house because they were all empty.

The gramophone was set going. The dancing began. People sang as they danced. What a noise there was! Everyone was excited and happy, because, set out at the end of the room, was a table full of good things. The four coloured jellies shivered and shook. The sugar rabbit on the iced cake stood up and looked with very sugary eyes at all the dancers. It was a very merry evening.

Blim-blam!

"Who can that be?" said Dumpy, in surprise.

Just as everyone was feeling hungry, and thinking it was about time the dancing stopped and the eating began, there came a knock at Dumpy's front door.

He opened the door. Outside stood someone dressed in a blue uniform, looking very stern.

"Hallo, Blueboy," said Dumpy, in surprise. "What do you want?"

"Have you any idea of the noise you are making?" said Blueboy, in a stern voice.

"Oh, we are only dancing and singing," said Dumpy. "We are not making much noise, Blueboy."

"And I say you *are*!" said Blueboy. "I could hear it very plainly indeed from outside. You may not be able to hear what the noise is like from inside. It sounds really *dreadful* out here! You will wake everyone up!"

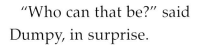

"But there is nobody to wake up," said Dumpy. "Everyone is here."

"Don't argue with me, Dumpy," said Blueboy, in such a cross voice that Dumpy was quite surprised. "I tell you that the noise from outside is simply dreadful."

"I'll come out and hear it," said Dumpy. He turned round and called to his guests. "The policeman says that the noise we are making sounds simply dreadful outside I'm going to hear it."

"You'd better *all* come and hear it!" said the policeman. "Then you will believe what I say. Come along, everyone!"

Blueboy went into the house and pushed everyone out. He shut the door – and once the door was shut, he took off his big helmet – and he wasn't Blueboy at all! He was naughty Tricky, who had dressed up as a policeman to play a joke on Dumpy!

He emptied the four lovely jellies into his helmet, and snatched the sugar rabbit off the cake. Then he slipped quietly out of the kitchen door and ran out of the back garden, home! He had been to the party after all!

The people outside crowded together and listened to hear the dreadful noise that Dumpy's party was supposed to have been making. They listened – and they listened.

"I can't hear a sound!" said Gobbo the pixie.

"Not a word!" said Tippy the gnome.

"The party isn't a bit noisy!" said Dumpy crossly. "I don't know what Blueboy meant. Why, there might be nobody in the house, it's so quiet! There's not a sound to be heard!"

"Well," said Happy the goblin, with a chuckle. "There *is* nobody in the house now – except Blueboy! We've all come out – to listen to ourselves making a noise indoors! Ho, ho, ho!"

"Ho, ho, ho!" roared everyone – and really, it *was* very funny, wasn't it! They had all gone outside to listen to the dreadful noise they were making *in*side! Dear, dear, dear, whatever next!

"Come on in," said Dumpy. "We'll tell that silly old Blueboy we didn't hear a sound!"

So into the house they all went – but where was Blueboy? Nowhere to be found! And where were the four beautiful jellies? Nowhere to be seen! And where, oh, where was that lovely sugar rabbit? He was gone – and the kitchen door was wide open! Oh dear!

"That wasn't Blueboy, it was Tricky!" suddenly cried Dumpy. "Yes, it was. I thought his voice wasn't Blueboy's. Oh, he has been to my party, as he said he would – and taken the best jellies – and my beautiful sugar rabbit too!"

"All because we were foolish enough to do what he told us – and leave the house to hear the noise we were making!" groaned Happy the goblin. "I know, Dumpy, let me run to Tricky's cottage and tell him we've found out his trick – and it was really very funny, you know – and say he can come to the party if he brings back the jellies and the sugar rabbit."

"All right," said Dumpy. "Go and tell him. He is too clever for me – I'd rather he was my friend than my enemy! Goodness knows what he would make us do next!"

clever trick you played, Tricky – but don't make Dumpy unhappy about his jellies and sugar rabbit. He was very proud of them!"

"Very well," said Tricky, getting up. "I'll come – and I'll bring the jellies and the rabbit with me!"

So Happy raced off to Tricky's cottage. Tricky had emptied the jellies out of his helmet on to a big dish and was just going to eat them.

"Hi, stop!" said Happy, running in. "We want you to come to the party. That was a

So back he went to the party with Happy – and everyone laughed and said he was a rascal, and Dumpy said he would forgive him if he wouldn't play any more tricks.

So they all settled down again, and the gramophone played, and the jellies were eaten, and the sugar rabbit was put back on the cake, where he looked simply splendid.

"It was a lovely party – even if the jellies *did* taste a bit helmety," said Tricky, when he said good-bye to Dumpy.

"Well – that was *your* fault!" said Dumpy with a grin.

Jinky the Jumping Frog

Jinky was a little green jumping frog who lived in the toy cupboard with all the other toys. He had a spring inside him that made him able to jump high up in the air, and he often frightened the toys with his enormous jumps. He didn't *mean* to frighten them, but, you see, he couldn't walk or run, so his only way of getting about was to jump.

"I'm sorry if I startle you," he said to the angry toys. "Please try and get used to my big hops. I can't do anything else, you see."

The toys thought he was silly. He was a shy little frog, and he didn't say much, so the toys thought him stupid. They left him out of all their games at night, and he was often very lonely when he sat in a corner of the toy cupboard and watched the toys playing with one of the nursery balls.

Now the prettiest and daintiest of all the toys was Silvertoes, the fairy doll. She was perfectly lovely, and she had a silver crown on her head, a frock of finest gauze that stood out all round her, a pair of shining silver wings, and a little silver wand, which she always carried in her right hand. Everyone loved her, and the green frog loved her most of all.

But she wouldn't even look at him! He had once made her jump by hopping suddenly down by her, and she had never forgiven him. So Jinky watched her from a distance and wished and wished she would smile at him just once. But she never did.

One night there was a bright moon outside, and the brownie who lived inside the apple tree just by the nursery window came and called the toys.

"Let's all go out into the garden and dance in the moonlight," he said. "It's lovely and warm, and we could have a fine time together."

Out went all the toys through the window! They climbed down the apple tree, and slid to the grass below. Then they began to dance in the moonlight. They all took partners except the green frog, who was left out. He sat patiently on the grass, watching the other toys, and wishing that he could dance too.

There was such a noise of talking and laughing that no-one noticed a strange throbbing sound up in the sky. No-one, that is, except the green frog. He heard it and he looked up. He saw a bright silver aeroplane, about as big as a rook, circling round and round above the lawn.

Then someone looked down from the aeroplane and Jinky shivered with fright – for who should it be but Sly-one, the gnome who lived in Bracken Country, far away. He was a sly and unpleasant person, and nobody, fairy or toy, liked to have anything to do with him.

"I wonder what he wants to come here for to-night!" said Jinky to himself. "He's up to some mischief, I'm sure!"

He was! He suddenly swooped down in his aeroplane, landed near the toys, ran up to the fairy doll, snatched her away from the teddy bear who was dancing with her, and ran off with her to his aeroplane!

How she screamed! "Help! Help! Oh, please save me, toys!"

The gnome felt quite safe in the air. He circled round and round the toys and bent over the side of his aeroplane to laugh at them.

"Ha, ha!" he said. "Put me in prison, did you say? Well, come and catch me!"

To the great anger of the toys he flew very low indeed, just above their heads. The teddy bear, who was tall, tried to jump up and hang on to the aeroplane, but he couldn't quite reach it. He was in despair.

The toys were so astonished that they stood and gaped at the bold gnome. He threw the fairy doll into his aeroplane, jumped in himself, and away he went into the air! Then the toys suddenly saw what was happening, and began to shout.

"You wicked gnome! Bring her back at once! We'll put you in prison if you don't!"

"Whatever shall we do?" he cried to the toys. "We can't possibly rescue the fairy doll in that horrid aeroplane."

"Ha, ha!" laughed the gnome again, swooping down to the toys – and just at that moment the green frog saw his chance! He would do a most ENORMOUS jump and see if he could leap right on to the aeroplane.

He jumped. My goodness me, what a leap that was! You should have seen him! He jumped right up into the air, and reached out his front feet for the aeroplane. And he just managed it! He hung on the tail of the plane, and then managed to scramble up. The gnome had not seen him.

The toys were too astonished to say a word. They stood with open mouths looking up at the brave green frog, and he signed to them to say nothing about him. He thought that if the gnome did not know he was there he might be able to rescue the fairy doll without much difficulty.

The gnome flew off in his aeroplane. He wanted to reach Bracken Cottage that night, and he meant to marry the fairy doll in the morning. He thought it would be lovely to have such a pretty creature cooking his dinner and mending his clothes.

The frog crouched down on the tail of the aeroplane. It was very cold there, but he didn't mind. He was simply delighted to think that he would have a chance to do something for the pretty fairy doll.

At last Sly-One arrived at Bracken Cottage. He glided down and landed in the big field at the back of his house. Out he jumped, and turned to the fairy doll, who was cold, frightened and miserable.

"Wait here a minute and I'll just go and unlock the door," he said. "Then I'll come back and fetch you." He ran off – and as soon as he had gone the green frog hopped down into the seat beside the fairy doll.

She nearly screamed with fright, but he stopped her. "Sh!" he said. "It's only me, Jinky the jumping frog. I've come to save you. Do you think we can fly back in this aeroplane?"

"Oh, Jinky, I'm so glad to see you," sobbed the poor doll. "Look, you jerk that handle up, and the aeroplane should fly up into the air."

Jinky jerked the handle in front of him, but nothing happened. The gnome had stopped the engine and, of course, it wouldn't move. Jinky was in despair. He didn't in the least know how to fly the plane, and he was terribly afraid that if it did begin to fly there would be an accident.

"It's no good," he said, hopping out of the seat. "I can't make it go. Come on, fairy doll, get out, and jump on my back. I'll leap off with you, and perhaps we can escape that way."

"Take the handle out of the aeroplane," said the doll. "Then the nasty gnome can't fly after us in it. He won't be able to make it go up!"

"Good idea!" said the frog, and he tore off the handle. He put it into his mouth, for he was afraid to throw it anywhere in case the gnome found it again. He thought he would carry it a little way and then throw it into a bush. The fairy doll climbed on to his back, and held tight.

"Now please, don't be frightened," said the jumping frog. "I shall jump high, but you will be quite safe. I can't walk or run, you know."

"*I* shan't be frightened," said the fairy doll, clinging to his back. "I think you are the dearest, bravest, handsomest, strongest frog that I ever saw!"

"Well! How Jinky swelled with pride when he heard that! He looked behind him to see that the gnome was still far away – but, oh my goodness, he was running back from his cottage at top speed, for he had seen the doll get out of the aeroplane!

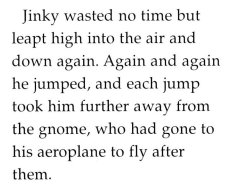

Jinky wasted no time but leapt high into the air and down again. Again and again he jumped, and each jump took him further away from the gnome, who had gone to his aeroplane to fly after them.

When he found that the starting handle had gone, he was very angry. He jumped out of the plane and ran to his garage. He opened the doors, and in a few moments Jinky heard the sound of a car engine roaring.

"Oh, my!" he thought in dismay. "If he comes after me in the car I shan't have any chance at all!"

On he went, leaping as far as he could each time. The fairy doll clung to him, and called to him to go faster still. Behind them came the gnome's car, driven at a fearful speed.

Then, crash! There came a tremendous noise, and Jinky turned round to see what had happened. The gnome had driven so fast round a corner that he had gone smash into a tree, and his car was broken to pieces. Sly-One jumped out unhurt, very angry indeed. He shook his fist at the jumping frog, and looked at his broken car. Then he ran to a cottage nearby and thumped at the door.

The sleepy gnome came, and asked him what he wanted.

"Lend me your bicycle," demanded the gnome. "I want to chase a wicked frog."

The goblin brought it out and the gnome jumped into the saddle. Off he pedalled at a furious rate after the frog and the doll.

"He's got a bicycle now!" shouted the fairy doll to Jinky. "Oh, hurry up, hurry up!" Jinky jumped as fast as he could, but the doll was heavy and he began to be afraid that he would never escape. Behind him came the gnome on the bicycle, ringing his bell loudly all the time.

Suddenly the frog came to a village, and in the middle of the street stood a policeman with red wings. He held out his hand to stop Jinky and the doll, but with a tremendous jump the frog leapt right over him and was at the other end of the village before the angry policeman knew what had happened. Then he heard the loud ringing of Sly-One's bicycle bell, and turned to stop the gnome. He held out his hand sternly.

But the gnome couldn't and wouldn't stop! He ran right into the astonished policeman, and knocked him flat on his face. Bump! The gnome flew off his bicycle and landed right in the middle of the duck pond nearby. The bicycle ran off by itself and smashed against a wall.

How angry that policeman was! He jumped to his feet and marched over to the gnome. "I arrest you for not stopping when I told you to, and for knocking me down," he said.

But the gnome slipped away from him, and ran down the street after the doll and the frog. The policeman ran after him, and off went the two, helter-skelter down the road.

The frog had quite a good start by now, and he was leaping for all he was worth. The doll was telling him all that had happened, and when he heard how the gnome had run into the policeman, he laughed so much that he got a stitch in his side and had to stop to rest.

"Oh, don't laugh!" begged the doll. "It really isn't funny. Do get on Jinky."

His stitch was soon better, and on he went again, while some way behind him panted the gnome and the policeman.

The frog felt sure he could jump faster than the gnome could run, so he wasn't so worried as he had been. For two more hours he jumped and jumped, and at last he came to the place where the toys had been dancing last night. They had all gone back to the nursery, very sad because they felt sure that the fairy doll and the frog were lost forever.

The frog jumped in at the window, and the fairy doll slid off his back. How the toys shouted with glee! How they praised the brave frog, and begged his pardon for the unkind things they had said and done to him. And you should have seen his face when the fairy doll suddenly threw her arms round his neck and kissed him! He was so pleased that he jumped all round the room for joy.

Suddenly there was a shout outside. It was the gnome still running, and the policeman after him! The gnome was so angry that he meant to run into the nursery and fight the jumping frog!

Then teddy bear did a clever thing. He put an empty box just underneath the window, and waited by it with the lid in his hands. The gnome jumped through the window straight into the box, and the bear clapped the lid down on him!

When the policeman came into the room too, the bear bowed gravely to him and handed him the box neatly tied round with string.

"Here is your prisoner," he said. "Please take him away, he is making such a noise."

The surprised policeman thanked the bear, bowed to the toys, and went out of the window again. Then the toys sat down and had a good laugh, but the one who laughed the loudest of all was Jinky, the little green frog!

Grumph the Rocking Horse

Grumph was an enormous rocking-horse and he lived in the middle of the nursery floor. He was a fine fellow with black spots all over him, a big mane, and a bushy black tail.

He rocked to and fro and took children for long rides. They all loved him – but the toys were afraid of him.

Sometimes he would begin to rock when they were playing about, and then, how they ran out of the way!

"Be careful, be careful!" they would cry.

"Tell us before you rock, Grumph! You might rock on one of us and hurt us badly!"

Then Grumph would laugh and think it was a great joke to scare the toys so much.

"You are not kind," the teddy bear said to him. "One day you will be sorry, Grumph." And so he was, as you will hear.

It happened that Billy and Betty had been playing with their toys one afternoon, and had left them all about the nursery when they had gone to bed. Nurse saw them there and was cross. "Those children will have to clear them up to-morrow morning!" she said, and she left them on the floor.

Now, the toy soldier's head and one of his hands were just under the rocker of the rocking-horse. He was quite safe unless Grumph suddenly rocked. The toys all watched anxiously, waiting for midnight to come so that they might rush out to the toy soldier and pull him out of danger.

Grumph chose that night to give the toys a scare. As soon as twelve o'clock began to strike, and he knew it was midnight, when all toys can come alive, Grumph began to rock.

"Stop! Stop!" shrieked the toys, running forward. "The toy soldier is underneath!"

But Grumph didn't listen. No, he thought the toys were scared as usual, and he didn't listen to what they said. To and fro he rocked – and the poor toy soldier was underneath!

Oh dear, oh dear, when the toys got to him, what a sight he was! His bearskin hat was all torn off, and his right hand was squashed to bits. The toys pulled him away and he began to cry.

"What's the matter?" asked Grumph, stopping and looking down.

"You wicked horse! We told you to stop! Now see what you've done!" cried the toys angrily. "You've torn off all the toy soldier's bearskin hat, and you've squashed his poor hand!"

The toy soldier was crying bitterly. Grumph was terribly upset – but it was done now! How he wished he had not been so unkind!

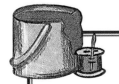

"What shall I do?" wailed the toy soldier. "Oh, what shall I do? When Billy and Betty see me, with my bearskin hat all torn off, and my hand squashed, they will throw me into the dustbin. Boo-hoo-hoo!"

"The rocking-horse had better take you to Santa Claus' workshop," said the teddy bear. "He knows the way because he came from there. He told me so. Perhaps Santa Claus can mend the toy soldier and make him better."

So the toys put the toy soldier on Grumph's back, and made him rock out of the nursery and down the garden towards the great hill where Santa Claus lived. It was miles away, and all through the night Grumph rocked hard, with the toy soldier on his back.

And at last he got there. Santa Claus heard the sound of his neighing and hrrumphing at the door and came to see who his visitor was.

Grumph explained, and the toy soldier showed his poor bearskin hat and squashed right hand. "Dear, dear!" said Santa Claus, looking severely at the rocking-horse. "I have heard of you and your stupid way of scaring the toys by rocking suddenly when they are near. Come in!"

The horse rocked in and Santa Claus took them to his workshop. He opened a drawer and looked into it.

"Dear me!" he said. "I've no bearskin left. It's all been used up. *Now* what am I to do?" He turned and looked at Grumph's mane. "You've a nice thick black mane!" he said, "I think you'll have to spare a little for the toy soldier!"

Then, to Grumph's horror, he took a pair of scissors and cut a big patch out of the horse's thick mane! How queer it looked!

Quickly and neatly, Santa Claus put the black hair on the toy soldier's head. He stuck it there with glue, and it soon dried. Then Santa looked at the toy soldier's squashed hand. He found a new hand and carefully put it on. It belonged to a doll, really, so it was pink, instead of black, and looked rather queer.

"Now I've no black paint!" said Santa in a vexed tone. "Only blue or red. Those won't do for a soldier's hand. Ha, Grumph! I'll have to take off one of your nice black spots, and use it for the soldier's hand. It will do nicely!"

He carefully scraped off a large spot on the horse's back, mixed it with a tiny drop of water and painted it on the toy soldier's new hand. It looked fine!

"Thank you very much indeed!" said the toy soldier, gratefully. "You are very kind."

"Not at all!" said Santa, beaming all over his big kind face. "I'm always ready to help toys, you know!"

Then off went Grumph home again, rocking hard all the way in order to get home by cockcrow. The toy soldier sat proudly on his back, glad of his new hat and new hand.

The toys cheered when they saw him. "What a glorious bearskin hat you have – and look at your fine new black hand!" they cried.

Grumph said nothing. He stood in the middle of the nursery floor, quite still, not a rock left in him.

"Santa took some of Grumph's hair for me, and one of Grumph's spots to paint my hand black," said the toy soldier. "You can see where he has a bare place on his mane, and one of his biggest spots is missing."

Sure enough, it was just as the toy soldier had said. The toys looked to see – and each of them thought that it served Grumph right.

And dear me, when Billy and Betty saw that Grumph had a bald place in his mane and one of his spots was missing, they *were* surprised. They couldn't think what had happened.

And now Grumph never scares the toys. He has certainly learnt his lesson!

Dame Thimble and her Matches

There was once an old woman called Dame Thimble who lighted her lamp as soon as it got dark each night. And every night she had to hunt for her matches. Sometimes they were on the mantelpiece, sometimes they were on the dresser, sometimes they were in the kitchen drawer and most often they were in the cupboard.

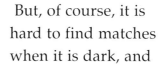

But, of course, it is hard to find matches when it is dark, and Dame Thimble bumped herself so often trying to find them that she decided to do something about it.

"I'll put them in my pocket in the morning," she said, "then when the evening comes I shall just have to put my hand in my pocket, and there I shall find the matches as easily as anything! I can light my lamp at once without hunting all over the place first!"

So in the morning she put the matches in her pocket, and then busied herself with her day's washing and ironing. She worked hard until tea-time, when she sat down and had a nice cup of tea. After tea she had to wash up and, as it was getting very dark by then, she wanted to light her lamp.

So she went to her cupboard to find her matches. They weren't there. Then she went to the kitchen dresser, but they weren't there either. Then she felt all along the mantelpiece and bumped her head on the corner of the bookcase nearby. But still she could find no matches.

"Yes, Dame Thimble, I will lend you some, but would you mind doing something for me in return? Would you go along the lane to the Bee-Woman's and ask her for a pot of honey? She said she would give me one to-day."

"Certainly," said Dame Thimble. So down the lane she went till she came to the Bee-Woman's hive-shaped cottage.

She knocked at the door and Bee-Woman opened it.

"They must be in the kitchen drawer!" she said, and off she went to look there, treading on the cat on her way, poor thing, and bumping her knee against the stool.

There were no matches in the drawer, though Dame Thimble felt at the back as well as at the front.

"I'll go and ask Mister Todd if he'll lend me a box," she said at last. "I can't *think* where mine are!" So off she went next door to Mister Todd's. He opened the door to Dame Thimble, and when he heard that she wanted some matches he nodded his head.

"Could you let me have the pot of honey you promised Mister Todd?" asked Dame Thimble.

"Oh Yes," said the Bee-Woman. "But I'll have to climb to my top shelf to get it. Would you go and ask Tompkins the cat who lives next door, to lend me his new ladder? Mine is broken."

"Very well," said the old dame, with a sigh, and off she went next door. Tompkins the cat opened the door to her and listened to what she wanted.

"Yes" he said. "I will lend the Bee-Woman my ladder, but I shall want something in return. Would you go down the lane and over the hill to where Diddle the Brownie lives and beg him to let me have a little of his fresh butter. I've quite run out of it to-day."

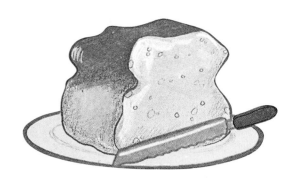

"I suppose I must, " said Dame Thimble, beginning to feel very tired. "I won't be long. Good-bye."

She walked all the way down the lane and over the hill to Diddle the Brownie's. She told him that Tompkins the cat had sent her to borrow a little fresh butter, and Diddle promised to get it from his dairy.

"Whilst I'm getting it, would you mind just popping next door to get a paper bag for it?" said Diddle. "I haven't one."

So Dame Thimble popped next door, and got a fine big paper bag from Tinkle the pixie, who, strangely enough, didn't want anything done in return!

Diddle put the butter into the paper bag and Dame Thimble took it, walked over the hill and up the lane, and at last came to the cottage of Tompkins the cat.

Then the old woman hurried to Mister Todd's cottage, and gave him the honey.

"Now, will you lend me some matches, Mister Todd?" she asked. "I really must have some to light my lamp."

He had fetched his ladder and gave it to Dame Thimble. She took it to the Bee-Woman, and helped her to raise it up to her top shelf. The Bee-Woman took down a small jar of honey from the shelf and handed it to Dame Thimble.

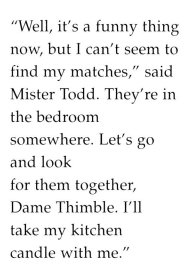

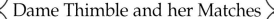

"Well, it's a funny thing now, but I can't seem to find my matches," said Mister Todd. They're in the bedroom somewhere. Let's go and look for them together, Dame Thimble. I'll take my kitchen candle with me."

So they went together into the bedroom, Mister Todd carrying his candle – but just as they entered the room the draught blew out the candle! And there they both were in the darkness.

"Well, *now* we're in a fix!" cried Mister Todd. "We shall go bumping into every-thing. Oh, dear, where can those matches be? We can't see to look for anything now. It's such a nuisance. We can't even light the candle till we've got some matches."

Now at that very moment Dame Thimble put her hand in her pocket, and what was her delight to feel a box of matches there! She took them out and struck one.

"Look, I've some matches in my pocket, Mister Todd! Now we can light the candle and hunt properly."

So they hunted with the lighted candle, but no matches could they find anywhere. Mister Todd got quite hot and bothered, and he took out his handkerchief to wipe his forehead – and out of his pocket fell – a box of matches!

"Oh, there they are!" he cried. "They were in my pocket all the time!"

"You stupid, silly creature!" cried Dame Thimble, quite losing her temper. "Here I've been going down on my hands and knees, poking in all the dusty corners of your bedroom and you had them in your pocket all the time! You are a big stupid, the biggest I've ever met. Fancy hunting all over the place for matches when they were in your pocket all the time! Why you didn't look there first I can't think! If I hadn't had *my* matches with me we couldn't even have lighted your candle!"

Mister Todd wiped his forehead and looked at Dame Thimble.

"Well," he said, "if you had your matches in your pocket all the time, why did you come here to borrow mine?"

Dame Thimble stared at Mister Todd. Dear me, what a very peculiar thing! Here she had been scolding him for doing exactly what she had done herself! She had popped her matches safely in her pocket so that she might find them easily, and then she had hunted all over her own cottage for them – which was just what Mister Todd had done. And she had called him stupid and silly, when she was just as bad herself!

"Oh my, oh my!" she groaned, sinking down into a chair, "I'm much sillier than you, Mister Todd. I've fetched honey from the Bee-Woman, a ladder from Tompkins the cat, a pat of butter from Diddle, and a paper bag from his next-door neighbour – and all because I didn't look in my pocket for my matches. I could cry, really I could!"

"No, don't do that," said Mister Todd, kindly. "Stay to supper with me instead, and we'll have hot cocoa and new bread and honey. You'd like that. We're two foolish people, so we ought to get on very well, and understand one another nicely."

So down they sat to hot cocoa and new bread and honey, and the very next week they got married – all because of a box of matches. Well, well, strange things do happen, don't they?

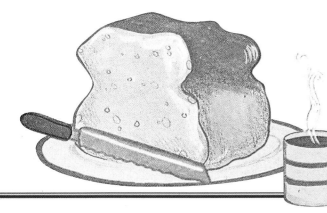

69

Enid Blyton

The Clever Toy Drum

Nobody in the toy cupboard liked the toy drum. For one thing it was rather big and took up a lot of room. And for another thing it made such a noise when the drum-sticks beat on the drum that all the dolls and animals were quite deafened.

"It's a noisy thing, that drum," said the toy soldier.

"It's too big for the toy cupboard," said the white teddy bear. "I shan't let it sleep here at night. I shall push it out on to the carpet!"

The white teddy bear was quite bold enough to do this, but the drum didn't wait to be pushed. Every night it quietly rolled itself out of the cupboard on to the carpet so as to give the toys more room, and stayed there all by itself. It was sad and lonely, for a drum likes jolly friends and chattering and noise – but it wouldn't push itself where it wasn't wanted.

"After all, I can't help being a drum," it thought puzzled. "I might have been a trumpet, or a toy soldier or even a white teddy bear. But I was made into a drum, and a drum must be round and it must make a noise."

Sometimes the drum tried to talk to Lucy Ann, the little golden-haired doll in the blue dress, who sat on a pretty chair just inside the toy cupboard. Lucy Ann didn't really mind the drum, but she pretended to be as grand as the others, and when the drum murmured a few words to her she turned her pretty back on it and wouldn't answer.

Then one night the toys decided to have a party. But they didn't ask the drum. Oh no! He was left out as usual. There were to be cakes, sandwiches and sweets, and afterwards the musical box had promised to play so the toys could dance. It would be a lovely party.

And then the toys discovered that they hadn't a doll's table big enough to put all the dishes on! So what do you think they did? Why, they pushed the drum into the

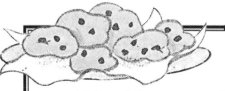

middle of the nursery floor, whisked a white table-cloth over him, and used him for a table!

They never even asked him if they might. He would do for a table, so he must put up with it, they thought. They giggled when they thought of him, sitting quietly under the table-cloth, holding all the lovely things to eat. Silly old drum! Only Lucy Ann, the golden-haired doll, felt a little bit sorry for him. But she didn't like to say anything.

The drum was so surprised when it felt the cloth whisked over him and the dishes set down on him that he couldn't say a word. He was very angry indeed.

It was too bad of the toys! They hadn't even asked him to the party, that was the worst of it. If they had asked him, he would have been pleased to help them and be their table – but they were unkind and they treated him as if he hadn't any feelings at all.

The drum had half a mind to get up and roll away, cloth, dishes and all! That would upset the toys finely and spoil their party! All the cakes would go rolling on to the floor, all the sandwiches would be upset. The drum really thought he would do it.

Then he thought of Lucy Ann. Perhaps she would cry if he played such an unkind trick. She wasn't very nice to him, but she was so pretty and so sweet that

the drum was really very fond of her. So he stayed still and let the toys use him for their table.

Now just as they were in the middle of their party, the nursery door was pushed open, and in came Scamp, the puppy! He had smelt the cakes and sandwiches and had come to see where they were. When he saw the toys there, sitting round the drum-table, eating, he was surprised. He bounded up to them and tried to push them away with his nose.

The toys jumped up, screaming. They took up the dishes of cakes and the plates of sandwiches and ran into the toy

cupboard with them. They knew how greedy the puppy was. They didn't like him a bit.

Scamp was angry when he saw the toys taking away the cakes and sandwiches. He snatched the cloth off the drum to see if there were any cakes under it. Then he ran into the toy cupboard and sniffed about for the sandwiches he knew were hidden there. When he couldn't find them (because the clever toy soldier had hidden them in the brick box and shut down the lid), he was angrier than ever.

He took up the toy soldier and shook him hard. Then he took the white teddy bear and tore off his nice blue ribbon. After that he nibbled some hair off the biggest doll and bit the tail off the poor frightened plush monkey.

What a to-do there was! The toys were crying and shouting, nearly frightened to death. Lucy Ann crouched in a corner of the cupboard, hoping and hoping that the puppy wouldn't see her. But he did. He dragged her out by her pretty blue frock, and she bumped her head against the toy cupboard.

Now all this time the drum stood outside watching. You might have thought that he would have been glad to see the unkind toys punished like this by the puppy – but he wasn't. No, he was worried and frightened. He didn't like to hear the toy soldier crying and he couldn't bear to see the white teddy bear without his nice blue ribbon. It was dreadful. The toy drum felt very sorry for all the toys.

Ah, but when he heard pretty little Lucy Ann, the golden-haired doll, crying in fright when the puppy pulled her out of the toy cupboard, then something happened to the drum. He began to think harder than ever he had in his life before, because he couldn't bear to hear Lucy Ann crying like that.

"I must get help, somehow!" thought the drum, anxiously. "Oh, how can I get help? It's no use rolling out of the nursery to fetch the children, because they sleep in too high a bed for me to reach them. What can I do?"

Then he had a wonderful idea! He would beat himself with his two drum-sticks, and that would surely wake up the children! So up leapt the two drum-sticks and began to beat the drum as loudly as they could. Rub-a-dub-dub! Rub-a-dub-dub! RUB-A-DUB-DUB!

Now Molly and Tony, the two children, were fast asleep in bed when the drum began to beat, for it was night-time and everyone was sleeping. But when the sound of the toy drum came into their dreams they both woke up in a hurry! They knew the sound of the drum very well indeed, for they beat it every day when they played soldiers.

"Listen, Tony," said Molly. "That's our drum! What's it sounding for? Let's go and see!"

Out of bed they jumped and ran into the day nursery – and when they had put on the light they saw that rascal of a puppy shaking the toys like rats!

"Oh you wicked fellow!" said Tony, smacking the puppy hard. "You know you ought to stay in your basket down in the kitchen all night. Go back to it at once!"

The puppy ran away quickly. The children stood and looked at the drum. It had stopped beating itself as soon as it had heard them coming, and was now quite silent.

"Who beat the drum, I wonder?" said Molly, astonished. "One of the toys must have done it to waken us."

"Isn't that strange?" said Tony, sleepily. "I wonder which toy it was, Molly.

Well, we've rescued them from Scamp, so we might as well go back to bed now. I'm so sleepy."

They went back to bed and left the toys alone. At first they were too upset and too frightened to speak. Then they sat and thought to themselves – and they thought about the clever, kind little drum, that had saved them from that dreadful rough puppy. The drum might have left them all to be nibbled and shaken – but it hadn't. It had called for help. It was a good-hearted drum, and a smart one too.

The toy soldier got up first. He went to the drum. "Please forgive me for having been unkind to you," he said. "I'm sorry."

"So am I," cried the white teddy bear.

"And so are we!" cried all the rest.

Lucy Ann, the golden-haired doll, ran to the drum and flung her arms around him.

"You're a darling!" she said. "You're cleverer and kinder than all the rest of us together. You shall be my friend!"

Well, think of that! The drum trembled with delight and didn't know what to say. Then the toys fetched out their cakes and sandwiches and gave another party, this time for the little toy drum. And always after that they were kind to him and made him their friend.

But he still likes pretty little Lucy Ann the best of all.

Enid Blyton

He Didn't Believe in Fairies

There was once a farmer who didn't believe in fairies. You should have heard him laugh when fairies were mentioned! Why, he almost deafened you!

Now I expect you have heard it said that only those who believe in the Little Folk ever see them. Those who *don't* believe in them can't see them even when they are right under their noses!

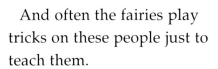

And often the fairies play tricks on these people just to teach them.

Farmer Straw only believed in horses, cows, sheep and things like that. If you mentioned such things as dragons, unicorns, witches or pixies he would explode with laughter and call you a ninny. The fairy folk used to listen, and they laughed too. It really *was* funny to them, you see, to think that people said they weren't there, when *they* knew quite well they were!

Now Farmer Straw had a very fine mushroom field. So had his neighbour. Farmer Twinkle, and his other neighbour, Dame Busy. And in the autumn they all got up very

early in the mornings and went mushrooming. When they sold their mushrooms in the market they made a great deal of money.

One night the little folk had had a dance in Dame Busy's field. It was a GRAND dance, with the grasshopper band playing rilloby-rill half the evening. That is the famous elfin tune, you know, that the grasshoppers know so well. There had been all kinds of games too, and a most delicious feast. And for once it hadn't ended at cockcrow, but just a little bit later.

Now this was a pity – because no sooner did the party break up than a rainstorm began! How it poured! How it pelted! The fairies, pixies and elves raced for the shelter of the mushrooms that had shot up in the night. They crouched beneath them and tried to keep their lovely frocks from being splashed. They hoped the rain would soon stop.

But it didn't. No, it went on and on and on. Goodness, the little folk couldn't possibly go home in it, they would be wet through! And see – there were lights in the farmhouses! People were getting up early to go mushrooming. Then what would happen to the fairies?

Dame Busy came out of her farmhouse with a big basket.

"Hey, little folk!" cried an elf. "We shall be caught here if Dame Busy arrives before we go. She believes in fairies, you know, so she'll see us here under the mushrooms. Let us quickly run to the mushrooms in the other field – those belonging to Farmer Twinkle."

So off the fairy folk scuttled through the wet grass and the rain, and soon they were safely sheltering under Farmer Twinkle's mushrooms. But dear me – it wasn't long before the farmer opened *his* farmhouse door and came out mushrooming too!

So off went the fairies again – this time to Farmer Straw's mushrooms. And bother me if *his* door didn't open and out he came, too, to go mushrooming!

"Our luck is out this morning!" cried an elf. "Whatever can we do? There are no more mushrooms to shelter us from this dreadful rainstorm! We shall have to go home and, oh dear, what colds we shall get, for we shall be soaked through!"

"No, don't let's get wet!" cried a pixie, "There's no need to! Let's each pick our mushroom and use it like the humans use umbrellas! We can carry them all the way home and never get wet at all! As for old Farmer Straw he won't see us for he doesn't believe in fairies! Ho ho!"

"Ho ho ho ho!" laughed all the little folk delightedly. Then they each picked a mushroom, and holding it above their bright little heads they made their way across the wet field down to the little wood where they lived.

Farmer Straw met them as he came to the field with his basket – yes, he met them – but he couldn't see the fairies, of course, because he didn't believe in them!

All he saw was a row of big mushrooms walking solemnly along in the rain! He stood and stared with his mouth wide open. Then he gave a scream of fright and ran back to his farm.

"Oh! Oh! I'm going mad! I've seen mushrooms walking! Oh, what shall I do?"

"Don't be so silly!" shouted Dame Busy and Farmer Twinkle. "It's only the little folk using them as umbrellas!"

"I don't believe in the fairies!" yelled Farmer Straw. "No, that I don't."

"Oh well, if you like to believe in mushrooms walking off by themselves, instead of in the little folk, you do as you like," said Dame Busy, scornfully. "But it seems to me to be much easier to believe in fairies than in walking mushrooms!"

Farmer Straw looked back at the row of bobbing mushrooms, half believing in the little folk for a moment – and just for that moment he saw a roguish face peeping at him from under a mushroom and caught a glint of a silver pair of wings. But it was gone in a flash.

"Only ninnies believe in fairies," he said. "I'm not a ninny. There's something gone wrong with my eyes this morning, that's all – or else I'm not properly awake yet. Ho – I'd rather believe in walking mushrooms than a dozen fairies! That I would!"

But I wouldn't. Would you? Anyway, Farmer Straw lost all his mushrooms that day and you should have heard the little folk laugh about it! Farmer Straw thought it was the swallows twittering – but it wasn't!

Enid Blyton

Sally Simple's Spectacles

Sally Simple had a fine pair of spectacles. They sat on her round nose beautifully, and looked very grand, for the glass was square, not round, and the frame was bright green. Sally Simple felt very fine indeed when she wore her spectacles. She didn't really need to wear any, for her eyes were perfectly good – but when she had seen those grand green spectacles in a shop, with their square glass, she had fallen in love with them and bought them!

One day Sally went to a sewing-meeting. She set off, in her best green blouse with yellow buttons, and her spectacles in a case. It was raining hard, so Sally put up her umbrella and went squelching through the mud.

There were a lot of people at the sewing-meeting. Old Dame Twinkle was there, and Mother Hubbard. Mrs. Pippitty was there and Mrs. Popoff. The meeting was quite crowded. Sally Simple was pleased.

"There will be all the more people to see my beautiful glasses," she thought to herself. She sat down at a table, and put her umbrella beside her, for she was always afraid that some one else might take it if she put it into the umbrella stand.

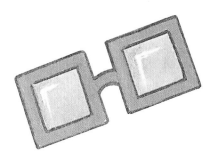

Sally took out her spectacle case and opened it. She put her marvellous green spectacles on her round nose and looked to see if anyone was admiring them.

"Goodness, Sally!" said Dame Twinkle, her shining face all over smiles. "What do you want spectacles for? Your eyes are as good as mine any day!"

"And what queer ones they are!" said Mother Hubbard.

"They cost a lot of money," said Sally Simple offended. "They are the very latest fashion. Your bonnet, Mother Hubbard, is much queerer than my spectacles. It must be more than fifty years old."

"Now, now!" said Mrs. Popoff. "No quarrelling, please. I am sure, Sally, that your spectacles will help you sew beautifully!"

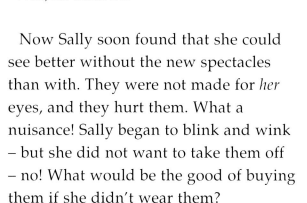

Sally put her glasses firmly on her nose and bent over her work. "Everyone is jealous of me because I have such fine spectacles," she thought. "Well, let them be!"

Now Sally soon found that she could see better without the new spectacles than with. They were not made for *her* eyes, and they hurt them. What a nuisance! Sally began to blink and wink – but she did not want to take them off – no! What would be the good of buying them if she didn't wear them?

But when tea-time came Sally Simple took them off and put them on the table. She did like to see properly all that she was eating. She ate tomato sandwiches and cucumber sandwiches. She ate brown bread and butter and strawberry jam. She ate a ginger bun, a chocolate cake, and two slices of cherry cake – and she drank four cups of tea. So she enjoyed herself very much, and laughed and joked with the rest.

But when tea was over, Sally thought she would put her beautiful glasses on again, and she looked for them – but, dear me, they were gone!

"I put them on the table, just here!" said Sally Simple, and she looked everywhere on the table for her lovely glasses. But they weren't there! She looked in the cotton box. She looked among the scissors. She unrolled the roll of cloth nearby. But nowhere could she see her precious glasses!

"Has somebody taken my glasses?" asked Sally in a loud voice. "They are gone! I simply must have them to wear whilst I am sewing."

"*I* haven't seen them," said Mother Hubbard.

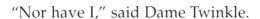

"Nor have I," said Dame Twinkle.

"I expect Sally's got them herself," said Mrs. Pippitty. "Have you looked in your pocket, Sally?"

"Of course, I have," said Sally. "I've looked everywhere!"

"They may be on the floor," said Mrs. Popoff. So everyone put down scissors, sewing, and needles, and hunted on the floor for Sally's' spectacles. But they were nowhere to be seen. It was really most mysterious. The empty case was in Sally's pocket – but the glasses seemed to have disappeared completely.

"There is only one thing I can think," said Sally, pursing her lips.

"And what is that?" asked Dame Twinkle.

"Well – I think *one* of you has taken my new spectacles," said Sally. "I know some people felt jealous of them! Now, who is it? I tell you, I really must have them back because they cost a lot of money."

"Sally! You should not say that one of us has taken your silly glasses," said Mother Hubbard crossly. "They are *not* silly," said Sally.

"They are – *very*!" said Mother Hubbard.

"They are *not*!" said Sally, going red.

"Now, now!" said Mrs. Popoff. "I expect they will turn up soon. Shall we all open our work-bags and see if the glasses have got there by mistake?"

So everyone opened her basket and tipped out cottons and silks and needles – but nobody had those glasses, it seemed. It was most peculiar. "Well, I simply don't know where they can have gone to, Sally," said Mrs. Pippitty. "Let us get on with our work again now. We have wasted quite enough time."

right up to her neck. She set her hat straight. She put on her gloves and buttoned them. Then she took her umbrella and walked to the door.

"Sally, don't go in a temper like this," said Mrs. Popoff kindly. "It is foolish of you. Your glasses will turn up somewhere, and then you will be sorry,"

"I shall *not* be sorry!" said Sally, who was most upset. She opened the door. It was pouring with rain. Dear, dear, what wet weather!

"And I hope that whoever has my glasses will be WELL PUNISHED!" said Sally. She opened her umbrella – and oh, my goodness me, out of it fell something that shone and glittered – something that fell to the ground – and smashed into a hundred shining little pieces – Sally's beautiful green glasses!

They had slipped off the table into her umbrella, as it stood by her knee at tea-time. No-one had thought of looking in Sally's own umbrella! Everyone stared and stared.

"Well, Sally," said Mother Hubbard, at last, "your wish has come true. You said that you hoped that whoever had your glasses would be well punished – and you were the one that had them – and you have been punished because they have broken."

"Well, I shall not stay here a minute more," said Sally Simple in a rage. "*Someone* has my glasses – my beautiful green glasses – and I shall go home and not come to this horrid, nasty sewing-meeting any more!"

"Don't be silly, Sally," said Mother Hubbard. But Sally's mind was made up. She was not going to stay and sew without her glasses! She got up from her seat and took down her mackintosh from its peg. She put it on, and buttoned it

Poor Sally Simple! She did feel so ashamed of herself – and there were her lovely glasses, smashed to bits – all because she had walked out in a temper! Tears poured down Sally's cheeks. Kind Mrs. Popoff saw them and came running to Sally. She put her arm around her.

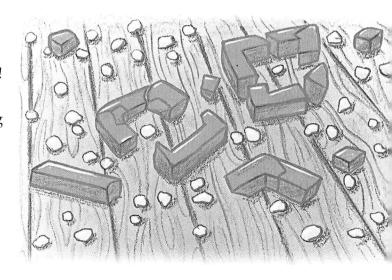

"Never mind," she said. "You look *so* much nicer without spectacles, Sally, dear. And besides, I am sure they were bad for your eyes, because they made you wink and blink. So don't worry any more. Come and take your things off again, and do a bit more sewing."

Sally was so ashamed of herself that all she wanted to do was to go home – but Mrs. Popoff was so kind that she went back again into the room and took off her things.

"I beg everybody's pardon," she said in a little voice. "It was very foolish and wrong of me."

And after that Sally Simple didn't buy any more spectacles – because her eyes really were very good indeed. She is much nicer now, so perhaps it was a good thing those green glasses were smashed to bits. What do *you* think?

The Beautiful Cricket Ball

The boys were going to play cricket. There were the twins, Peter and John, Alec, Tom, Jim, Fred, Ian, and Hugh. What fun it would be!

"We will play on that nice smooth stretch of sand!" said Peter. "You put the stumps in, John!"

Little Harry came running up. "Peter, Peter!" he cried. "Can I play too?"

"No," said Peter. "You're too small."

"But I can run fast," said Harry. "Oh, do let me play, Peter. I won't ask to bat – just let me field for you."

"No, we've got enough players," said Peter. "Run along and play with your sister, Harry."

Harry was very disappointed. He had so hoped to play cricket with the big boys. It would have been such fun. He could run very fast and, although he didn't bat very well, he could bowl quite straight.

He went off, hurt and sad. Peter might have given him a chance!

His little sister was building a castle. "Come and help, Harry," she said. Harry took up his spade and began to dig. It was no good being horrid to Susan just because someone had been horrid to *him*!

The boys drove in the stumps – and then Fred brought out a most beautiful new cricket ball.

"Look, boys," he said. "Here's a fine ball! I had it for my birthday yesterday!"

"My!" said Peter and the others, looking at the beautiful ball admiringly. "That's a beauty! Can we play with it to-day, Fred?"

"Yes," said Fred, proudly. "But will you let me bat first if I let you play with my new ball?"

"All right," said the others. "Take the bat, Fred. Who's going to bowl? You, John! See if you can get Fred out with his own ball?"

The game began. Harry, still digging castles, could hear the click of the ball against the bat as Fred drove it over the sand and then ran. The boys shouted. They ran after the ball and threw it in. John stopped bowling and Ian began. It all looked very jolly indeed, and Harry wished and wished he could have played too.

At last Fred was bowled out. He gave up the bat to Peter, who was a very good batsman indeed. Hugh took the fine new ball to bowl to Peter. It felt so good as he twirled it about – the best ball the boys had ever had to play with!

Hugh bowled, and Peter struck out. The ball flew along the sand, and Peter ran, and ran and ran. He meant to make more runs than anyone else that morning! At last the ball was thrown in again and Hugh caught it. He bowled it to Peter again. Peter slashed out with the bat. Click! Went the ball. The ball flew towards the rocks.

"Stop it, Ian, stop it!" yelled Fred. "Don't let it go among the rocks, or we shall lose it."

But Ian could not stop it, for the ball was going too fast. It rolled fast towards the rocks. It struck once and flew up into the air – then it dropped somewhere.

"Find it, find it, Ian!" yelled everyone.

"Hurry! Peter is making more runs than anyone!"

Ian hunted round the rocks. He could not see the ball anywhere. How he hunted! He looked under the seaweed. He looked in every pool. That beautiful new ball was not to be seen!

At last the others came to help him look too. They peered here and there, they splashed into the pools, but it wasn't a bit of good – that ball could *not* be found!

"It's gone," said Fred, very much upset. "Quite disappeared. What shall we do?"

"Better play with our old one," said John. So the old one was got out and the game went on. But everyone was very sad about Fred's fine new ball. It was too bad to lose it the very first game.

Harry had been digging all the time the boys were hunting for the ball. He didn't like to go near them, for he was afraid they would send him away again. He did not know whether they had found the ball or not – but when he saw them playing again he thought they must have found their ball. He didn't know it was the old one.

The castle was finished at last. Susan wanted to do something else. "Let's go shrimping," she said.

"All right," said Harry. "We'll catch some shrimps for your tea, Susan."

They took their shrimping nets and went to the rockpools. They pushed their nets through the sand and looked to see how many shrimps they had caught.

"Only one tiny crab," said Susan, and she and Harry put their nets in the water again.

"I can see a big prawn!" suddenly shouted Harry, in delight. "Hurrah! Come here into my net, prawn!" But the prawn would not be caught. He darted here and there, and at last disappeared under a shelving rock that jutted out into the pool. Harry stuck his net under the rock to catch the prawn.

He drew his net out and looked into it – no – there was no prawn there!

"Harry, something rolled out from under that rock when you stuck your net there," said Susan, pointing. "What was it?"

Harry looked down into the pool. He saw a big red ball there. He picked it up. "It must have been under that ledge of rock," he said. "And when I poked my

net underneath it must have made the ball roll out. I wonder whose ball it is."

"It belongs to those boys," said Susan. "I heard them say they hadn't found their ball. They are playing with another one."

"Are they really, Susan?" said Harry. "This must be Fred's beautiful new ball then. He must have been upset when it couldn't be found."

"Are you going to take it back to them?" asked Susan.

"I don't know, " said Harry. "They were horrid to me this morning. I don't see why I should be nice to them."

"But Fred will be so sad if he doesn't get his new ball back," said kind-hearted Susan. "Don't you remember how bad we felt when we lost our new kite, Harry?"

"Yes," said Harry. "All right, I'll take it back to the boys."

He dried the ball on a towel, and then ran to where the boys were playing. He waited until the batsman was bowled out and then yelled to Peter:

"Peter! I've found Fred's new ball! It was in the rock-pool, catch!"

The boys turned in surprise. Fred gave a cheer. "Hurrah! I'm so glad!"

Peter caught the ball and stared at Harry. "That's jolly good of you," he said. "You are a sport! I say, boys, what about letting him come into the game? He must be a good sort to bring back our ball when we wouldn't let him play this morning!"

"Yes, let him come!" roared all the boys. "Come on, young

94

Harry! We'll let you play with us. It was decent of you to give back our ball!"

So Harry joined the game – and wasn't he pleased and proud. He fields very well indeed and, do you know, although he only made one run, he bowled out Ian and Hugh. The boys were quite surprised.

"You play a good game, Harry," said Peter, at the end. "You can come and play with us again to-morrow."

Now Harry always plays cricket with the big boys – and how glad he is that he took Susan's advice and was nice to the boys when he really didn't want to be! As for Fred's beautiful new ball, they are still playing with it. Its stay in the rock-pool didn't hurt it a bit!